Wallaby Booth

Joanna Weaver
Illustrated by Tony Kenyon

To John Michael Weaver:
I couldn't imagine having
a more wonderful son!

Faith Kids® is an imprint of Cook Communications Ministries,
Colorado Springs, Colorado 80918
Cook Communications, Paris, Ontario
Kingsway Communications, Eastbourne, England

WALLABY BOOTH
© 2001 by Joanna Weaver for text and Tony Kenyon for illustrations

Editor: Kathy Davis
Graphic Design: Granite Design
First printing, 2001
Printed in Singapore
05 04 03 02 01   5 4 3 2 1

This book belongs to:

_____

"The Lord detests lying lips,
but he delights in men who are truthful."
Proverbs 12:22 (NIV)

There once was a boy named Wallaby Booth
who struggled a bit when it came to the truth.
It wasn't that Wallaby wanted to lie.
  "It's just that the truth is so boring," he'd sigh.

His dad owned a business
       called Stan's Laundromat.
But according to Wallaby,
       he was much more than that.
"Don't tell," he would whisper,
       "my dad is a spy.
Why, he knows more secrets
       than the whole FBI!"

Then he'd tell them a story and fill it with glory
    till all of his friends were amazed.
He so stretched the truth, did our Wallaby Booth,
    that his friends just stood there and gazed.

So that's how my dad saved the world with three hangers and a purple striped tie.

Soon Wallaby's boasting
    and bragging backfired,
for all of his friends
    and his buddies grew tired
of Wallaby's need
    to be biggest and best,
to be grander and greater
    than all of the rest.

The more he'd exaggerate, the easier it became
to make up a story than take any blame.
"Where is your homework?" his teacher would ask.
"And if you don't mind,
would you stick to the facts?"

"It was terrible, Mr. Barclay," little Wallaby would say.
 "A tornado came 'long and just swept it away."
"The wind came a'swirling, the pages went whirling.
 They flew right out of my hand.
The wind opened the door, and it blew 'cross the floor,
 blowing my homework as far as Thailand."
"Is that really the truth?" Mr. Barclay would prod.
 "I have to be honest, it sounds very odd."

"W-w-well . . ." the boy stuttered. "I guess that it's not.
I was watching 'Space Rangers' and sort of forgot."

Soon no one would listen when their friend told a story,
for he'd won a spot in the "liar" category.

So when he said, "Hey, guys! You'll never believe it . . ."
   they all said, "Of course not! Come on guys, let's beat it."
"But my uncle is coming
   from Australia, down under.

My uncle Bob is a famous outback guide and he's been in movies and . . .

He's bringing his crocodile,
 Samuel O'Gunder!"
"Yeah, right!" his friends muttered
 as they all walked away.
"Come see him," Wallaby yelled.
 "He'll be here Saturday!"

But when Saturday came,
    Wallaby Booth sat alone.
His friends didn't come
    and his friends didn't phone.
"I don't know what happened,"
    he told his dear uncle.
"Where are they?" he wondered,
    his face all a'rumple.

But then the phone rang.
　　It was Sidney, next door.
"Hey, wanna go with me
　　downtown to the store?"

"I can't," replied Wallaby.
    "My uncle is here."
"Yeah right, I believe you,"
    Sidney said with a sneer.

"I'm telling the truth!
    Come and see for yourself."
Then Wallaby hung up
    the phone on the shelf.

Before very long the whole gang was there.
   They all looked surprised as they stood everywhere.
"Your uncle is here with his pet crocodile!
   I can hardly believe it," Sidney said with a smile.

"I don't blame you," said Wallaby, "with the lies that I've told.
Who would believe me? My fibs must get old.
From now on I'll be truthful. (Oh, please help me, God.)
I will not exaggerate or be a big fraud."

"Will you forgive me?" he asked, ducking his head.
"Of course we will, silly!" they all gladly said.

"Wallaby Booth, we're telling the truth,"
    his friends said, taking the cue.
"It's not where you go, or the people you know.
    We like you because you are you!"

"C'mon, mates!" said Uncle Bob. "Enough of this talk.
Let's go to the beach and take Sam for a walk."
"Yeehaw!" yelled the guys, and they let loose a cheer,
while Wallaby grinned and wiped 'way a tear.

They spent the whole day
    throwing Bob's boomerang,
Wallaby, Sidney,
    and all of the gang.

"It's good to have friends,"
    Wallaby said with a smile.
Then he gave them high-fives
    and hugged the reptile.

Faith Parenting Guide

Ages: 4-7

Life Issue: My child is learning to be truthful.

Spiritual Building Block: Honesty

Learning Styles

Help your child learn about God's Word in the following ways:

Sight: Read with your child the Scripture passage in the front of this book: "The Lord detests lying lips, but he delights in men who are truthful," (Psalm 12:22). Be sure your child understands the difference between "detests" and "delights." Ask your child to find a picture in the book in which the Lord would detest what Wallaby was saying. Then ask him or her to find a picture showing Wallaby telling the truth, which would delight the Lord.

Sound: Ask your child: Which of Wallaby's stories are lies and which are the truth? Discuss why Wallaby tells lies (to impress his friends, to get out of trouble, to sound like he is better than others). Ask: What happens when you lie (people stop believing you, even when you tell the truth)? Ask if your child has ever had a friend who told lies or exaggerated the truth. Is it difficult now to trust this friend?

Touch: Play this guessing game with your child. Collect a dozen crayons and put them in a paper bag. Have your child close his or her eyes—no peeking! One by one, place the crayons in your child's hand and announce the color, deliberately lying about some. See if your child can guess when your are lying and when you are telling the truth. Ask: What does lying do to the trust between people? (It destroys it.)